BANG! BANG! BANG! Not the first thing I wanted to hear on my 25th birthday, but at least someone is excited, I guess. My older brother is out at the moment, most likely studying, but should be back within the next few hours. BANG BANG BANG! "CALM DOWN, I JUST GOT UP!" I shout. Who has the audacity to bang on my door on MY DAY?? After I finish getting dressed, I finally work my way to the door.

"Yes?" As I swing the door open, at least four people aim their spears at me.

"We were calm long enough, now since you took so long, we want anything and everything you have," said one stranger at my door. To be honest, they wouldn't find much in this crappy shack, but I don't really feel like them thrashing the place.

"I'll give you a fair warning, but if you stay, it's your problem-" the robber swiftly removes my head with a spear, cutting my sentence short. My body drops limp on the floor just a few inches away from my head. They step over my body, laughing and cursing how crappy of a dump my place is as they're scavenging for anything. As they're going through, my head rolls back towards the rest of my body and I regain full control.

"You guys could really use a lesson in manners."

I leave the strangers bewildered, unable to finish their sentences. Before they can respond, I swiftly take down three of them and warn the remaining one to leave if he doesn't want to suffer the same fate as his friends. Nodding, he takes his buddies with him, and I witness them leaving the town. The sun is almost at its peak, which means I have a fight in about 30 minutes. Not one of these disorganized fights, but an actual structured, regulated match. I leave a note for my brother and venture off to my bout. I'm told they have something special for my birthday fight and I'm just getting more excited. Through extensive travels across the southern world and along the Silk Road, I've mastered diverse fighting styles. I'm constantly captivated by the agility of new fighters and eager to learn how to adjust accordingly. Regardless of the outcome, I hope to have an enjoyable time.

The sun glaring through the trees as I enter this trashy mud hole into this hut. I've been to multiple different fighting pits around, but this was the first one I ever stepped in, where I grew up. I've been able to meet fighters from all over the world, some of them even offering me a chance to come to their home place and learn their ways. Through the fights, I've learned of many martial arts from across the world, but there's still more I want to know.

"CALM DOWN, NO ONE CAN UNDERSTAND YOU LADY!!!" I hear yelling from the desk. Is it a newcomer? Maybe I should go check it out. When I get there, there's a woman towering over the man behind the desk. She must be at least 6'5" and have darker skin, but she's not from here judging by her way of speaking.

"I said I want my sword back. My idiot brother had bet it on his best friend and he told me I would have to travel into a shanty dump to get it back. 愚かな兄弟 always having to clean his mess…" Her brother…oh, she must mean Uso. He said he was from Japan and that he wasn't much of a fighter, but his friends and family studied to be Samurai or something like that. Now that I think about it, the reason she lost her sword is kind of my fault. Maybe I can clear things up with no hostility.

"You there, what do you want?" she chimes in, noticing me before I can get my thoughts in order.

"I may or may not have been the one to get your sword sold by accident." I responded.

She furrows her brow. "Are you saying they bet on you and lost my sword?"

"No, they bet against me and lost, but I'm sure I know who has the sword now and I'm willing they'd have a match for it."

"Alright," she clears her throat, "find me out the culprit and I will face them in the arena." It took me off guard. I was the reason she's in this predicament.

"Please, don't worry about it. I can handle it for you," but before I can finish, she bursts in.

"Nonsense. All you did was something you're accustomed to. The one to blame is myself for not paying attention to my weapons and letting my brother snatch it. Plus, I'd like to test my new sword I had made before arriving here." I can't really say anything to stop her so I bring her to the catering area and, of course, the man I thought who'd have it is flaunting it off, Dawit. He boasts about anything that he takes even the smallest amount of pride in, whether he did it, and usually it comes with him betting on me in the ring. He used to get beat up all the time when we were just kids, the bigger kids constantly pushing him around just for being smaller than average. I could've intervened, but I thought to myself that it had nothing to do with me. One kid tried to push me around one day, and all I did was a small shove, but it sent him flying. Everyone had heard about it and ever since then, Dawit has been following me around since, but that doesn't mean he's a pushover. It's almost as if he has a natural ability to mimic other's movements as he's gotten older. He likes to match up against me, but he hasn't won, yet every time I have to change my entire fighting style because he practically copies a fighter, he's seen my face in the ring.

This time, though, this woman is going to face him in his first proper match. When she challenged him, he seemed all but too eager.

"There's only one person who could beat me in a fight, so I'll even let you make the rules." Dawit states confidently.

She scoffs, "fine, the only rule is we use the sword we have on hand with us right now."

"Obviously, I have this one, but where's yours?" As he says this, a glyph appears directly to the woman's right, and she pulls out a Katana with a purple blade and a wooden handle that is in the shape of a snake's head.

"My name is Chairoi Ruju and I will take back what's mine!"

It's about 3 minutes before the match begins, and I do still feel like Dawit has her sword because of me, so I decide to discuss some things.

"So, just to let you know, we don't kill here." Chai gives me a stink face.

"And why not?" she asks.

"Because I said so," I say confidently. She paces around a bit, but then sighs and responds.

"Fine, I will spare him. But he won't satisfy me unless he puts up a proper fight!" she declares boldly.

"My gift to you. If you win, I'll fight you." I say.

She stares at me, examining me up and down before saying, "I know my brother lost a bet that he made against you. I thought he might have just made a silly mistake and judged poorly, but I can feel that there's an aura you give off that's not exactly human. It has piqued my interest." Her serious face turns into a promiscuous grin. "I'll fight you after I'm done with this, and hopefully some more later."

I don't understand it myself, but my soul is telling me I need to fight her to see if I've grown myself. Usually, I'd be overconfident in those around me, but right now, I'm worried about everyone, especially Dawit.

The door opens. "Ms. Chairoi, are you ready?" One guard questions.

"As ready as I'll ever be. Well, Mr. Zakary, I hope you keep a close eye on me." As she says this, she lifts her left arm up and gives me a salute. She wore a sleeve on her entire arm and had black gloves on, but I could tell she was hinting about something with it. I rush out to the spectators' seats but am stopped by the owner, Kibiri. He asked me to sit with him and give my opinion on the matchup.

"Well, sir, Dawit is no slouch. He spars with me often and has been flourishing, but there's something about this woman that irks me. She's not normal."

He laughs, "So wouldn't that make her more like you? How would you like to go up against her after this, anyhow?" Funny how that works. Whether she wins or loses, he'll give me the fight I want.

I responded, "only if she wins, and wants this fight to be a private match. Charge as much as you want for it."

"Ooh, perfect. Both participants will get at least 20% each. Sounds fair?"

"Yes, of course," the match is starting, so I ignore Mr. Kibiri. Dawit comes out with her Katana. I didn't notice before, but it looks like it has a small rabbit talisman at the bottom. Its sleek silver blade shines with the white insignia shimmering off the lights in the arena. I never noticed how well Dawit was taking care of it. I guess Chairoi could appreciate that much.

"I'm not gonna lie. I'd be pretty upset if I had to part ways with such a beauty, but the sword I won't miss that much," Dawit chuckles.

Chairoi laughs, "You'd be lucky to tickle me, boy, but I appreciate how well you've been taking care of my toys. I'll leave you with a small scar to remember me by."

As she says this, she rips off her sleeve and shows off her prosthetic arm. I've seen nothing like it. It almost looks like it's from another planet, but then I remember what her brother, Uso, had told me he had been traveling to learn about replacement limbs. There was a story of a poor man that was once a renowned doctor whose king fell ill. The doctors in the land told the king that they would have to amputate his arm to stay alive and this made the king quite distraught and even quick to anger because of his disfigurement. The poor man used scraps of metals and leather to make a prosthetic arm for the king and he even got him to move it like a real arm, but no one was sure what he did exactly to do that. Looking at Chai's arm, though, I think I see the answer. Right at where the arm ends, and the metal begins, there's a blue-ish green aura that I've only seen when my brother would sew animal's limbs back together to nurse them to health. I didn't realize you could use the same spells on false body parts. Interesting.

"If there is one thing my brother is useful for, it's his medical ingenuity. Now, let's get started."

In the same instance she finished speaking, she disappeared. And then, right above Dawit, she came swinging down. STINKT! Split second reaction from Dawit, saving the match from being over at the start. Whatever she did just now wasn't something a normal person could do. I've seen nothing like it.

She chuckles. "I guess you're quicker than I thought." Dawit doesn't have any sort of retort. He's usually high and mighty, but this time, you can tell he's hyper focused. He's determined to show the fruits of his training not just to us around, but to his own self as well.

Chairoi, noticing this, scoffs, "Guess it's time to get serious." She readjusts her metal arm and gives off a gust of steam. They both take a stance and draw their swords. Staring one another down, testing to see who will attack first. Dawit braces, which signals Chairoi to leap forward, stabbing directly at his chest, but he can dodge it and throw a counter swing Chai blocks. Her metal arm shoots out air as she swings around and hits him in the side with her elbow. As he grunts down, she kicks him back, and he tumbles away, slowly regaining his footing. She has too much natural strength compared to him, regardless of the arm.

As he takes back his stance, she points her sword at him, taunting. "Is that it?" Dawit hasn't bitten yet, and he isn't backing down now.

She sees this and is getting annoyed. "Fine, I'll just end it now." She digs some dirt up and tosses it in the air. As it's falling, she readies her stance, clenching her sword as if it was being pulled out its sheath. When it hits the ground, she's already on the other side of the arena, behind Dawit, who stands there in awe. He falls onto the ground, unconscious.

"Don't worry, he's fine. I hit him with the hilt." Chai clarifies. The bell dings as the medicinal staff run to check on Dawit. Chairoi picks up her sword and scans the arena to find me.

"So, when do you want to start our match?" She asks eagerly, hopping on her tippy toes, keeping herself ready. I don't even know how to respond. The fight ended with an attack that I don't think anyone could see.

"Give me like 10 minutes so I can check on Dawit, too." I say.

She sighs, "Understandable, take your time. I'll be waiting by the ring." I rush to check on Dawit, who seems to be awake but just left in a daze.

"How are you holding up, buddy?" I ask.

He looks over at me, leans up and places his hand on my shoulder, "listen, you aren't ready for her yet."

I'm surprised. "Are you kidding me? Just cause she can move fast doesn't mean she'll be-"

"NO!" He cuts me off and tenses, grabbing his ribcage. "It wasn't just that she's fast. When she hit me, it felt like I had an entire building land on top of me."

"Do you think it had anything to do with her arm?" I ask.

He shakes his head, slowly recovering from his injuries and picking himself up. "I don't think it's that. The arm is impressive. I don't think I've seen any craftsmanship like it, but she didn't hit me with that arm. When she jumped towards me, I saw it for a split second. She switched blade hands and was using her real arm."

Is…is that even possible? I've met no one stronger than me, but it sounds like Chairoi might be in a league of their own, like my brother. Maybe I can learn from this, especially if I fail.

"Chai!" I shout as I approach her.

She turns her head and smiles when she sees me running towards her. "Soo, you ready?"

"Yea, I'm also curious. How do you feel about a hand-to-hand fight?" I ask.

"Hmm," she paces back and forth for a bit, looking at her sword that she had just won back. "I don't see why not. I need to brush back up on my Taekkyon."

"Taekkyon?" I say in a curious tone.

She giggles, "Yea, I can't use just some random stuff against you. I gotta show you my best work." She walks away and wishes me luck while I sit there wondering what the hell is Taekkyon?? I've only ever done basic boxing and grappling with mixes here and there. I guess other fighters have been using other styles, but have never said the name, so maybe someone has fought me with this style, but I just never heard the name before. The best option is to just be prepared for anything. This match was supposed to be private, but because of how many people will pay, it became a city-wide event, apparently.

As I'm getting into the ring, Chai wants to make a bet. "If I win, come back with me to Mount Kita and train."

"That doesn't sound like a punishment t-"

"AND, you have to do all my chores and call me 'Sensei', agreed?" she adds.

Ugh, I definitely would rather not...however, "If I win instead, open up a school here to teach your 'Taekkyon', deal?"

She shrugs. "I'm not exactly an expert at it yet, but deal." We let them know we're ready, bow and take our stances across one another. I feel my mind racing as I think about the techniques she will use and how much power she will output, but before I know it, the gong rings and she lands a swift kick in my chest, which pushes me to the ground and knocks the air out of me. If I had been a normal human, maybe I wouldn't be able to get back up so fast, but I think she can tell I'm not normal. I get up as fast as possible and try to read her next moves. This is the first time she's kicked in a match, so I guess this has something to do with the Taekkyon. Maybe it's primarily focused on kicks and knees instead of punches and elbows?

"By the way," she cuts off my train of thought, "this fighting style is all about how cool the attacks look, so get ready!" Based on how 'cool' the attack looks? Surely this couldn't beat someone in a fight then, right? As I'm thinking this, she literally flies in at me with a front flip and almost lands a kick square in my face with me just barely able to block it. I don't know what this is, but every attack she throws feels like a rhino is trying to run me over. As she's trying to gather herself back, she leaves herself open. I go in for a grab to sweep her down, but she reverses it and throws me over her shoulder. As she pins me on the ground, she wraps her legs around my arm to put it in a submission hold. I know this could get bad, but instead of trying to break out of it, I stand up and try to slam her down, but as the steam bursts out of her arm, I realize she won't let go soon, so I have to figure out some other way out of this.

I try to slip my other hand through the small crevice and it works, separating us as we both take steps back to gather ourselves. Grappling won't work and she has the strength and reach advantage with her height. I'm at a loss here. The only thing I can do now is try to make it interesting. I rush in at her with no thoughts, and she grins and runs towards me head on as well. She jumps in the air and kicks.

I duck under and swing an uppercut towards her, but she dodges my fist, and uses my arm to wrap and slam me down to the ground.

"Are you done yet?" She questions, while preparing to hit me with another blow if I don't yield.

"...How's the food at Mount Kita?"

Well, this isn't how I expected my birthday to go. After gathering stuff for the trip, I let my older brother know I'll probably be back in 6 months.

"I also have a question, though."

He looks up from his books. "Is it about magic?"

"In a sense, yes. Remember how you told me that if we ever fought seriously, I'd win because I'm more spirit attuned? How do I beat someone who has both?"

He pauses for a second to think.

My older brother, Chimer, he's been studying magic and the history of the world since before I was born. His magic has become so powerful that he could realistically take out an entire army with the wave of his hand, but part of that is because of how much research and patience he has to do all this studying.

"Alright," he exhales, "I know how to answer your problem. So remember this primarily, it's a Rock-Paper-Scissors system with it going in this order: Magic-Spirit-Technology. But, just because it's a system like that doesn't mean you can't mix it up together."

"You mean like rock would usually lose to paper, but you put spikes on the rock and now it cuts through?"

"Exactly. You told me that this girl used martial arts, but she also had a prosthetic arm that was also infused with magic. You claim to not lose because of it, but I had a raven watching the fight, and I noticed she tired you out with the arm bar you couldn't get out of, which she put you in with said prosthetic arm." I try to defend her and say it was all fair, but he stops me and tells me he understands that.

"I'm not worried about that, but you can be in a serious situation that you're against someone you can't beat with just raw strength, and it puts those around you in jeopardy. Remember, I know what you are, but you have to understand your own limits and figure out new solutions to problems, right?" I nod. "Alright, since you're going to be leaving soon though, take this book with you."

He tosses me a book on basic spell-casting, and I ask, "you want me to practice in my spare time, I'm guessing?"

"Well, you're going to need to learn at least basic magic to mix it into your own fighting style if you want to be one of the strongest in the world." He responds. I guess he's right. Some of these spells apparently are supposed to cast familiars, so I think I'll practice that and see how far and for how long they stay manifested for.

I tell him I'll see him later and go on my way, saying bye to the rest of the villagers and then meeting up with Chairoi who is waiting at the bridge for me. "So you all set?"

"One moment," I tell her as I pull out the spell book and look for the familiar page. For newer mages, say the spell to cast it. More experienced mages have built up mana pools to where they can cast whatever their pool can provide.

"Acinonyx Jubatus!" A glow of ethereal blue light appears on the ground, slowly rising, revealing the animal I summoned being a cheetah.

Chai looks at me and spouts, "Interesting trick, but wouldn't a horse or something have been more useful?"

"That's my exact thought," someone said. We both jump back and draw our weapons to search around for whoever that was. "SHOW YOURSELF!"

"Oh, I apologize, let me explain," the cheetah approaches me and says. "I am a manifestation of your magical essence." I just didn't expect this.

"This actually isn't too often that familiars from first time magic users can speak. It usually happens on the third try when they screw up and give us a missing eye or an overgrown toenail."

Chai and I are both surprised, but then she asks, "If it's okay with you, can we possibly ride on your back?"" The cheetah stretches, yawning, walks around and then nods, beckoning us to hop on. I didn't realize just how long this cheetah is. It seems more like a tiger with its length.

"I assure you, I am, in fact, a cheetah," he says, reassuring me. I guess since it's my magic, it can also read my mind. "A question though, what's my name?"

"How does Xander sound?" He scoffs, "you couldn't use a normal name like John? Is it at least with a Z?"

Chai cuts in. "X sounds better."

Xander growls, "ugh, whatever, Xander it is, I suppose. Now hold on tight because I am about as fast as a cheetah would be, so we'll be out of this city sooner than expected!" Saddles pop up underneath us with ropes to hold on to and belt straps, to keep us extra safe. Before I even realize, we're zooming unbelievably fast.

We left around noon last night. It's early dusk, and Xander is going headstrong out of the Sahara. Apparently, familiars can stay awake as long as needed. They don't disappear just because you go to sleep. Another bit of information I found out while reading on this trek is that familiars can also exist far away from their initial host. Size is the only limiting factor. The furthest an adult dragon familiar has been from its host is about 90 kilometers, but most others can be up to about 1700 kilometers in range. Kind of fascinating to think about and even more amazing how they apparently don't let up on their primary task until it's completed or we need to take a detour. On our second day, we arrived in Baghdad, Iraq, to trade with the local vendors. I need to get some heavier clothes for the mountains and Chai was getting irritable, not having that much to eat for this trip. They had people from all over trading here, some being just from a town over, others being from far-away lands, but all coming together to trade cultures.

As I'm looking for clothes, I bump into a young woman. "I'm sorry, ma'am."

"Don't worry about it," she responds, obviously trying not to make eye contact.

"Uh, if you wouldn't mind, could you help me out?"

She hesitates, then turns around and asks, "what is it you need?" When she turns around, she looks at me directly, and it's as if I'm mesmerized. Her hair is wavy and brown, her skin is a smooth olive tone with freckles on her cheeks, her lips are plump, and her eyes are two separate colors. One is dark brown, but the other is an amazing tone of blue. It's so bright and vibrant that it practically radiates. However, upon inspection, it seems as if someone cut the eye. "Are you okay?" I ask.

My curiosity peaked, and she noticed me staring, quickly covering her cut eye. "It's fine. Nothing a stranger needs to worry about. Is this what you needed help with?"

I snapped back, "I'm sorry. I meant I was wondering if you knew where I could get a coat for colder weather."

She sighs, and beckons me, "you're in the wrong shop. It'll take us a bit to get there, but I can bring you to what you're looking for."

"Thank you!" I say, trailing close behind her. I try to use this bit of time to make conversation, but she keeps ignoring me. Nothing seemed to work until I asked where she's from. She stops dead in her tracks, "I…I'm not sure. I believe it was a city called Beirut, but I remember little of the outside back then."

"What do you mean?" I ask.

She turns to me. "I didn't exactly have much freedom until a few years ago, to be honest. Just being outside right now is amazing, feeling the air brace my skin, seeing the sunlight. I never want it to end."

BANG! BANG! BANG! The loud noise scares me more than the men around me taking me away. My mom told me she had an enormous gift for my 5th birthday, but I didn't know she meant she was sending me away. She didn't like that I studied so much and focused on learning instead of helping them get money to pay off my papa's debt. Before my papa died, he would tell me I was his special scholar, but now I'm just afraid I won't be able to do anything.

It's been three years now. Other than just normal work things, the stuff these men have done to me, I don't even want to describe. I feel so gross every time I wake up. I can't take a bath alone. They send the other girls in to take baths, and then a large amount of men join us, touching all over us. It doesn't matter when we say no, to them it only means to be more aggressive. One man I had said no to got so upset, he took a knife to me and cut my eye, so now I'm half blind. I just miss papa and home.

On my 12th birthday, the men had given me the same present my mother gave me, so I was being auctioned off again. I've basically given up on anything at this point. It feels like my life couldn't get worse than it is, and I wish someone wouldn't monitor me all the time so I could end it all now. Living is nothing but hell. I'm auctioned off to someone that gives triple the gold that was offered, so I guess it's nice that someone is saying I'm worth so much, but I couldn't care less. I just want to get this over with. As we leave the building, and are in a private place, the stranger takes off their hood. To my surprise, it's the first woman I've seen that hasn't been getting tossed around like a doll. She says that she wants to "help me, heal me." When we arrive at her home, she sends me to the bath. It's…nice. No one barging in, no one trying to peek in or touch all over me. So this is what privacy feels like. It's soothing. After I get out of the shower, the woman says she has a gift for me. I panic. They sent the last two gifts to an auction. I JUST GOT HERE! There's no way I'm losing this home. I run to the room and slam the door, holding it shut.

I yell at her, "I'M NOT GOING ANYWHERE! YOU CAN'T TAKE ME BACK TO THOSE MEN!" Without even realizing it, I'm on the ground, crying my eyes out. I haven't cried since I first left with the men when I was only 5. I kept trying to be strong, but all those years, all those…things they did, I can't handle it. The thought of it makes me just finally break down. She pulls the door over and hugs me, whispering that it will all be okay and it's over now. Her arms are so soft and warm, it's nurturing. It feels like I'm back in my papa's arms again. I miss you…papa…

The sun beams through the window on my face, waking me up. When I open my eyes, though, it feels strange. My vision has improved. Then I realize, my eye, IT'S BACK! But how? Did it just get like, plopped back in or something? Wait, the woman, is she still here? Maybe she knows what happened. I ran to look for her, finding her cooking in the kitchen. "Uh, what's your name?"

She cackles, "Oh, I'm sorry sweetie, I must've forgotten my name a long time ago. You can just call me Baba, though. What can I call you though, my love?"

"M-my name is Alba."

She stops cooking to come to me. "Alba is a beautiful name. How do you like your new eye, Alba?" I put my hand over it, still trying to become readjusted to it.

"Yea," I asked, "how did I, uh, grow this?"

"You didn't exactly grow it, sweetie," she says, sitting me down and offering me some bread. I've never had someone willingly offer me food. This is a first. She explains that she's a witch and shows me her tomes.

It's amazing. I never thought something like magic was real. "Could you teach me how to use magic?"

"Of course, Alba, I've been looking for a protégé for a long time now, so you could be the perfect candidate. Also, about your eye, when the time is right, you'll know." When the time is right? My eyes? This is a lot to take in, but at least I get to learn magic!

It's been about a year, and my magic has been getting along steadily. Baba taught me about mana pools and familiars, and I learned that I have a larger than normal mana pool. I also found out there's a loophole you can do with familiars. If you summon a large animal and then break them down into a smaller animal, you can have multiple familiars instead of the one you are usually allowed. It's as if they split their own consciousness. The only downside is that they lose their speaking abilities, but other than that, there are no drawbacks. There's a room that remains locked since before I arrived, and I've been having familiar fairies attempt to open the door for the past two weeks. It was initially just 4 of the 20 I made trying to break the lock, but now, I only have about 3 left around me. I'm more surprised that Baba has said nothing about it, but if she's not turning an eye, then I should be in the clear. One fairy from the room came flying to me on my day off, telling me to hurry to the door. I rushed over to see that they did it! They broke the lock and opened the door! I see what secrets are in here, waiting for something to mesmerize me, and what I find is…nothing. Just a pile of clothes, an enormous pile, but still. Wait a minute, this seems like children's clothes, too small to even fit me. Baba doesn't seem like she'd be having a child soon. I hear loud banging steps coming up behind, "ALBA!" I hear Baba screaming in the distance, with me panicking, I try to hide under the clothes, the familiars going into hiding as well.

"Alba, I'm not mad. I wanted to explain, but I didn't know when the time would be right." How could she explain this? Did she need to have a kid that died early? Maybe it was someone's gift, and she actually is pregnant. I decide to come out, and I call her name.

"Alba, sweetie, I'm sorry for not telling you sooner," she sighs, hugging me. "I'm confused Baba. What do you have to be sorry for?"

"I didn't tell you the truth. There's a reason I'm so proficient in my magic. When I was younger, the best magicians were only good at simple things like party tricks, and pulling animals out of hats. But there were sorcerers in secret who studied for years, and one of their tricks was to make things immortal."

"Immortal? What does that mean?"

"It means to live forever. You see, I'm a lot older than my body gives off, but that will soon change my love." She grabs my hands, holding them tight. "when I was a younger woman, I had bought children, but children that didn't have any parents left specifically. If they don't have any family left, then who could miss them? I thought. To extend my life, I used the life essence of those kids. I was born in the year 775 in the Göktürk Empire."

I let go of her hand, slowly backing away. "You said you used kids without parents because you assumed no one would miss them. So are you saying no one would miss me, either?"

"No, sweetie-"

"DON'T SWEETIE ME! I trusted you. You just admitted you killed children."

"AND I'M TRYING TO MAKE UP FOR IT!" she snaps back at me, making me jump. She's never yelled at me before, because she knows it makes me feel like I'm back in those slumps.

Baba apologizes for the outburst, stating, "I promise you, I wanted to go back and stop myself from doing it countless times. But I found out the unfortunate way you can't go back. I found out though, there is a way to go forward, and I want to help push you forward into being a much, MUCH better version of me than I could have ever been." She doesn't seem to bluff, and even though what she did was a terrible thing to do, I can't help but forgive her since she saved me from my own horrible circumstances. If she didn't treat me the way she did and she had just wanted me for her own youth, then I probably would've just given myself up, to be honest. And maybe she's right, nobody would have missed me.

"Okay. I believe you. I just want no more secrets between us anymore, agreed Baba?" She smiles, and hugs me, "agreed my love."

It's been 4 years and every year, Baba's health has been getting worse, up to this point. She can barely speak and I've been taking care of her lately. Over the past few years, I've gotten slightly better at interacting with others, and I'm not as scared of men anymore, especially because I know I can protect myself now. My magic had gotten so powerful, I believe I could have overpowered Baba when she was younger. As I'm making stew, a fairy comes to alert me to Baba. Her health is deteriorating fast, with no way to stop it. She's been so infused with magic that she fades away, turning to dust. It's a terrible thing for me to think about. I won't have anything to bury, because she'll be gone in the wind.

Before she goes entirely, she says her last words, "Alba, you have all the knowledge I could give you. You know what to do, my love, and I will always be with you. I love you, my sweet daughter, Alba." This is the first time she actually called me her daughter. I always thought of her as a mom, but her dying words calling me family make me feel…special. A year ago, we talked about goals in life, and she said other than having a family, her goal was to show people how their future was before it happened and give them the option to change it. She had entire recipes to create an elixir to give to witch or wizard with enough mana and they would cast the spell to cover the planet, infusing it with everyone in the world, and making it a part of our DNA strands. It would be so powerful that even a fetus could comprehend and decide as if they were already a full-grown adult. I wonder though, would I have still picked to live through my life if I had the option at birth? The recipe includes ingredients from all around, so I don't think I could go scavenging just yet, maybe in a few years. I rested for today to think back on my memories of my mom, Baba.

A month has passed, and I just keep thinking back on what she said, "you know what to do." Is that supposed to be a message? I scurried all around the house and saw nothing until I went back into that "locked" room. While searching through the heap of clothes, an unknown substance unexpectedly splattered into my right eye, setting off an intense, fiery pain. I've felt nothing like this before. In my desperate attempt to find relief, I'm running to any water source and kicking and screaming. I run outside, trying to get to the river, and then get pushed down. A group of men surround me and are asking me if I'm okay. I don't think they mean any harm, so I just tell them I'm all good and try to go on my way, but then one man grabs my arm and says he can make sure I'm okay if I go home with him. I don't know where his friends are, but now I'm stuck with this and I'm too focused on my eye to cast any spells to stop him.

Suddenly, though, everything around me freezes. The clouds stop moving; the water doesn't flow anymore. I can't break out of the man's grip, but he stops pulling and I notice something in front of me. It's as if 3 pages are in front of me, but these 3 pages are moving, showing me the scenario I'm in. But it seems like 3 different outcomes? I'm so confused. One outcome shows the man pulling me, but a group of women intervene, chasing him off. The Second outcome shows the man just letting go and running away.

And the third outcome shows the man's friends coming back to tell him to stop, and he lets me go but he says, "you got off easy for now." I don't really want to deal with other people right now, and I don't like his response in the third option, so my only proper choice is two. By tapping on the picture, everything suddenly snaps back. I glare back at the man to let me go, and he does, running as if he saw the most ferocious beast of his life. That was strange, and my right eye stopped burning as well. I was planning on running to the nearest doctor, but it seemed to work itself out, so I headed back home. Is this what Baba meant when she said that I would know when the time was right? I think I'll give it a year, see how this little 'choice' thing goes and then decide if I should leave or not then.

A year has passed since the incident, but I understand what Baba had meant. I've been able to use this new 'power' a bit more willingly now, and even figured out how it works. It was on a 4 hour time limit: If I had used it once in the limit, I'd have to wait before I could use it again. I learned, however, as I've been growing with my magic mastery and getting into better physical shape, the time limit has decreased and I've been able to use it now every hour and a half. There have been rumors going around about a monster living in the city, but apparently whenever people cross paths with them, they're too afraid to speak about it and just try to forget about it completely. With the looks I've been getting, I'm assuming they're talking about me. It's probably based on how my powers work. I think if I make them just run from me, they see me as this all-powerful entity, but if it makes them leave me alone, that's all that matters. I need to figure out what I have to do exactly to fulfill Baba's dream. According to her books, there is a green crystal in an eastern country. That has to be crushed and minced into this soup, along with stuff from Baba's hometown that she had instructions to retrieve. There was a spell to freeze things in time and she froze the ingredients, an interesting spell. I wonder if it could work on other things like humans. Leaving tonight seems like the best option, since it's still early in the morning and some of the other villagers would be confused if they saw me walking out of here with this big bag.

As the night falls, I pack my things and get ready to leave, but before I can, strange men with torches surround my house.

"We heard the old witch that used to live here is gone, but assumed those were just rumors. We came to burn everything down, but didn't know anyone else stayed here." This has to be a joke, right? They want to burn down the only proper home I ever had? Yea Baba may not have been a super noble woman, but she redeemed herself, right? My chest pounds, my head is spinning and I feel myself get weak, but then I take a deep breath and open my eyes. Most of the time, I tie the power with my emotions, but I've figured out how to fuel it through certain emotions and forcefully release it. My hatred for everyone helped it come out even better. These people don't know what I had to go through. My choices seem basically identical, and the last thing I see is that man from the other day. The entire group disperses, saying they must've made a mistake, but he's just standing there on every single one of my visions, and then it goes gray. I might as well just confront it. Everything goes as is, and he stays his ground. I wait to see if he does literally anything at all. For a solid minute of silence, he finally takes a step forward.

"You…" He says, slowly getting closer. "You're the girl from the other day."

"If you're smart, you wouldn't take another step." I threaten him to back up, but he runs, pulling out a dagger. How pathetic. I raise my hand and he's lifted from the ground. "What the hell???" This is strange. My eye feels like it is ice cold now and my vision gets reddish.

"It's hot…Why the hell is it so hot??" The guy I'm holding in the air is writhing in pain. I drop him and scream at him to get lost. That's strange. It's like something was adding extra firepower to me. Is it from the eye Baba gave me?

"Oh."

There is a sharp pain in my side. I look down to see the dagger sticking in my abdomen and now I'm being dragged by my hair. I was so busy trying to figure out what happened that I wasn't paying attention to anything around me and that piece of crap got in close.

"LET ME GO!" I yell, but then I get kicked in the back of my head.

"SHUT UP!" This is bringing back unwanted memories. Being abused, dragged, I'm guessing he's trying to take me back somewhere to do god knows what. I feel like my eyes are watering. I haven't had to deal with any genuine conflict like this. Baba would always keep me out of this kind of situation. Everything is getting blurry. I just want to be rescued. "Baba, please…save me."

When I wake back up, there's a trail of blood on the ground. It's not mine. I even seemed to be patched up with bandages for my wound. I follow the trail and I wish I had just turned away. The man, or what remains of him, is left there, with body parts scattered everywhere. It's as if he had exploded from the inside or something. Just looking at him makes me want to vomit, but it's even worse because apparently he's not dead.

His head, which is sitting on a counter, says, "you did this to me." What the hell is he on about? How could I even manage something as horrific as this? "You did this to me, you monster. JUST KILL ME! PLEASE, I CAN'T LIVE LIKE THIS!!" I grab my stuff and run as fast as I can out of there. How could I manage something like that? Someone else must have done that. I don't even remember anything after passing out. And now that I think of it, maybe that monster deserves it. Who knows how many more girls he would've done that too if I hadn't been there? The thought of it pisses me off so much. You know what? I need to do one more thing. I don't run too far off from the house to where I can't see it, before turning around and casting a spell I learned to 'light a candle" as Baba would say. Usually it would just be used for that, but I wonder if I can make it work on a larger scale. I cast the spell with as much power as I could, and the entire house turned into a damn candle. That's what he deserves, nothing less. As I leave, I wonder if I really did that to him. If that's the case, just how strong am I, actually? I was worried I wouldn't be able to do this task, Baba asked, but maybe she picked the right person! Don't worry Baba, I'll make sure our dreams come true and no one ever has to suffer again.

"Hey…HEY! You've been standing here for a while, lady. What are you doing, reminiscing?" I'm pretty sure she was just daydreaming, but it's been 7 minutes already. What is this chick's deal? I can't get a read on her at all.

"Sorry, and don't call me lady, please. You can call me Alba."

Oh, finally a name, "Name's Zak, you said you're from Beirut? My friend I'm with was there before she came to my village."

"Your friend? If it's a man, then he'd probably be scum." What's that supposed to mean? "Well, she's not the play-"

"SHE?? Let me meet her after we find you the clothes." Seems like her mood changed when she found out it's a woman.

As we're scouring through the clothes, I ask her, "Considering you called men scum, why didn't you react to me as scum when I bumped you?" As she grabs a coat with fur at the top, she comes to me to measure if it's my size and answers, "you have a particular feeling to you. I've only felt it from two people: Baba and my father. You give off a nourishing feeling, as if there's nothing to worry about near you."

A...nourishing feeling? Did she say I feel like a parent? I guess that could explain why it's so easy for me to talk to people.

She hands the coat, "this looks like it will be good on you, let's go quick, I want to meet your friend." It's amazing, before Alba's face was bleak, but now she's so excited to meet Chai, her smile is radiating and her eyes are shining. Her other eye was blue before, but now it seems as if it's greenish-blue.

"Alba, I forgot to tell you- "

"THERE YOU ARE!" Chai cuts me off as she runs towards us, towering over me already. I'd say Alba is roughly around 5'2, so Chairoi stands more than a foot over her, looking down and asking, "who's this?"

Alba's eye turns to black quickly, catching Chai's attention. "Did your eyes just change colors? THAT IS SO COOL!"

The black turns to a yellowish-orange, and she calms down a bit and responds to Chai, "yes, I learn my eye will alter depending on my feelings towards certain situations. Some colors have multiple meanings, though, so it could be the same color for two polar opposite reactions. I've also found that my iris will have different forms depending on those same emotions."

I've heard of this before. Wizards and witches with special body augmentations will have those areas glow, especially if they're also infused with magic.

"So that eye isn't your original eye, right?"

"Correct," she responds. "Baba gave it to me a long time ago. It was a gift to help remember her."

Her eye becomes a somber pink.

"We don't have to talk about such a serious topic," Chai butts in. "Where are you headed after you leave this place?"

She responds, "I'm not sure. Apparently, there's something that's supposed to lead me to 'where I'm supposed to be'. It's a rare mineral, so rare that it's believed to be fictional, but Baba would never lie to me."

Chai scoffs, "well you seem to have a lot of respect for this Baba, so let's see if she's right. Where do you want to look?"

Alba reaches into her bag and pulls out a map. "Baba left this for me. She used to travel with a group on the seas, and as she was, she would use magic crows to scan the area, so she made a map of the world she discovered. This is where we are, in the eastern section of the map." The map seemed to have included my home as well, but was outdated since it said Aksum, even though the kingdom isn't what it used to be.

She continues, "we need to go here to find the mineral and it should take about 9-10 days to get there."

"You must be talking about on horseback or something of the sort," Chairoi chimes in.

"Yes, I could tell by your energy that you have been exerting a substantial amount of magic before arriving here, so I was hoping you could accompany me?"

I don't really feel like taking any more detours, even though she seems like a genuine and great person. I feel like she'd be fine if I refused. "It doesn't sound like it'd be in our best interest. I just- Sounds great, meet us at the gate." It should serve as an interesting experience in a new environment, and me and Chairoi could use the downtime.

Wait, something just now felt a bit off. I don't know how to describe it exactly, but I just know that something is off. "Great, I'll see you guys then in about an hour and a half," Alba says as she walks away.

"Zak..." Chairoi calls out to me with shakiness in her voice. I look over and to my surprise, her arm is back entirely. There's actually no trace of any metal. Her entire arm is back as if it was never gone.

"WHAT THE HELL HAPPENED??"

"I DON'T KNOW, I'm so confused," she yells back. This couldn't get any weirder. It feels like something just got flipped on its head and somehow, Alba causes this.

"Zakary, I need to spar. I haven't had flesh on this side for a while, so I need to make sure it's not gonna fall off the second I use any attack of force." She makes a fair point, and if Alba can do things to our bodies without us even noticing. Then maybe it's best to always be on edge, especially since she's going to be traveling with us.

"Alright, but where are we going to spar?"

"We are literally in a desert. We can just go somewhere far out since we still have an hour and a half, no?" So we rode Xander about 4 minutes away from the gate off the main trail to avoid attracting spectators. Chimer pointed to a particular spell in the book that created a barrier. The barrier trapped everything inside and would only collapse if the caster released it or became incapacitated. Since we want to see how much her arm can handle, this might be necessary. After setting the stage, we stretch to make 1000% sure that the ligaments aren't somehow fake, but almost breaking it backwards while doing exercises, it is definitely the real deal.

"Alright," Chai calls out, "I'm ready. Let's get started!" We take our stances and she lunges forward with a strong right jab that breezes past me. I duck just in time to dodge, but it's good to see that the speed hasn't changed. No, if anything, she's even faster now since she doesn't have to slug around a metallic arm. I try to counter with an uppercut, but she dodges and clocks me on the chin with a backflip. Damn, she's adjusted fast to it and is still just as flexible as before. It's amazing. I've never seen her move so fluidly. As the sparring match went on, it felt less like a fight and more like a dance. Before she was all brute force, hitting you like a lion. She still was agile, but it was her power that had more focus. But right now, it's her swift, fluid movements, dodging as if her body is moving on its own. Landing softly and moving in a slow and methodical pattern, but with such speed and ferocity that you have to be ready for the next strike. After about an hour of our sparring session, we sat down outside the gate and relaxed. Chairoi broke the silence asking, "What do you think that girl's intentions are?"

"What do you mean?" I responded.

"Ok, so," she sits up to explain, "isn't it weird how we meet a girl with some strange eye situation, that I'm pretty sure has SOMETHING to do with magic, and then we have that conversation about meeting up here, and then, BAM! My arm is back. Not strange at all to you?"

I think to myself a bit; it is strange. "Well, considering you usually hide your arm, whatever happened, someone probably didn't have any knowledge of it, and because of the lack of knowledge, it led to them inadvertently helping you."

"That would make sense." Chai says. "When I went to check it, there weren't even any metallic scraps left, though. That's what threw me off. My entire arm up to my shoulder was gone until a little over an hour ago. Cleaning up that mess would require more than magic."

Before we could go into any further detail about it, Alba arrives. Both Chai and I had discussed leaving before she would notice, but it was almost as if there was a barrier and we were being forced to stay somewhere easily reachable by her on foot. "Greetings friends," she says warningly to me and Chairoi. I don't understand how, but every time she appears in front of her, I'm entranced.

I struggle to look away for even a second, and Chai notices. "Hey, maybe keep the ogling down to a minimum?"

"My apologies. I don't know what's happening."

Alba reassures me it's ok. "It's probably because of my eye still, it has a charming effect on people."

"Yea, something like that." I try to shrug it off, but there's something else that I can't explain yet. I called Xander out to give us a ride.

"That's what you've been using?" Alba scoffs . "Do you have something bigger we can use?"

"As a matter of fact, I do. That's a novice spell, but I've been practicing for years, so I have spells that an average human won't be able to even comprehend. But we're special." As she finishes her sentence, she begins the spell. She generates a swirling green aura from beneath her, and a silhouette emerges, lifting her off the ground. Once the silhouette finishes forming, a jade dragon appears with the aura bursting off as it roars.

Xander switches to a bird and whispers to me, "Yeah, maybe this was a good idea to bring her along." Me and Chai board the dragon and tell Alba what direction to go, and before we know it, we're off.

I ask, "So does yours talk?"

"Excuse me?" Alba says in a confused tone.

"Your dragon, does it talk? Xander, mine talks all the time. It can get annoying."

"Yes, it talks, but usually telepathically, since it's part of my conscience. It doesn't enjoy sharing its opinions with outsiders." Interesting, I guess mine is more vocal because I'm an interactive person.

"On another note, how long will it take for us to get to our destination?"

"Not sure," Alba replies, "it's not only based on our destination, which I only have a general idea of where that is, but I also have to conserve energy because casting this behemoth drains me, and it's not even at its full speed. If I went to max speed, it would probably take us less than a day, but I won't be able to move for a week."

"Damn, that's rough. Let us know when you want to do some pit stops. Then we can look around and see if there are any taverns below." I guess for now, there's nothing much we can do about our situation but enjoy the ride.

After about 9 hours of our voyage, we see a thunderstorm coming towards us, and we'd rather not be the first ones getting pelted by rain since we're so high up, so we decide to land. Luckily for us, the city we stopped just outside of seems to have some sort of party happening. When we arrive, it's as if there was a big event that just happened, but I'm not sure what the language is. Luckily, there's a beginner spell that every new mage learns, especially if they plan to travel, called "silver tongue". You cast it, then once you hear one word from someone else's language, it essentially floods the entire language into your brain and then you can speak it and understand it, and you'll still hear whatever your original language is. The only downside is you can only hold up to 5 languages at a time, so I'm going to have to get rid of French for this one. I go up to one of the audience members. "Excuse me, what's going on here?"

" ਇਹ ਇੱਕ ਨਾਟਕ ਹੈ ਮੇਰੇ ਦੋਸਤ!"

There we go, "I'm sorry, what did you say?" He responds, "I said, it is a play, my friend! And a most jovial one at that!" I see, there were never many plays at home, but we had performers come in whenever we needed extra money for the club. I think the best option right now for us is to just find somewhere to rest up, though, especially since Chai and Alba are waiting and conversing.

"Do you know where the nearest place to rest is?"

"Of course," He stands up to help redirect me, "you'll go out those doors, and it's the second building, friend."

"Thank you, sir." I head back out to Chai and Alba to help them gather their things. "So, what have you guys gathered about where we are?"

I question the girls. Alba answers, "we're in Kashmir according to the locals. It's been a very knowledgeable time here recently with one of their most prolific philosophers passing not too long ago, so they practice his teachings often."

I respond, "you got all that from your first conversation?"

"Yes, it seems this place is very inviting, but it may be its downfall. Apparently, they are also rather fond of the religion known as Hindu."

"Ugh, of course it's a beacon here," Chai heckles. "Isn't Buddhism and Hinduism following the same teachings?"

"Barely. I guess if you believe in things like karma or reincarnation, but they believe in the caste system. It's why most of my family stays on the mountains on my father's side. My mother came from a wealthy royal family that are Hindu practitioners. I still love her, but I just can't look at her the same as when she left us and told us why." We arrive at the Inn and I offer to get three rooms, but Chai and Alba insist they'll share, so I get two for us to spend at least 2 nights here. Getting to my room, this is the first time I have been able to actually wind down and soak everything in. This is the first time I've been this far from home, and also traveling with two incredibly strong and incredibly beautiful women. Yea, I don't get the motive of one of them and the other one is so much fun to fight and watch her fight, but still. I guess I should probably get some sleep, though.

It's dark. I open my eyes and notice I'm in a cave or somewhere that has water covering everywhere but leaving my face with room for me to lie down, yet still breathing freely. The only exit that I can see is the opening on the roof that is providing the small amount of light I have. I'm confused. How did I get here? I would panic more, but I feel too at ease and this is one of the safest spots I've been in for a while now. Maybe I can wait a little longer…

"ZAK!" a woman's voice echoes, jolting me up from my rest. I surveyed the area, but the room was still as dark and the sound didn't come from the roof's opening.

"Who is calling me?" I responded. After a moment of silence, they call back, "Zak, you need to wake up."

"Wake up. What are you on about?"

"I'm speaking to you telepathically. I saw you were asleep, so I made you lucid dream so I could speak to you. It's Alba. We HAVE TO GO! There are guards coming to your door. Me and Chai are already out. Use the window if you want to avoid them, but we need to leave, HURRY!"

This being a dream makes more sense, but she forced my brain to activate during the dream. Is that what she said? How the hell is that possible? Well, the current task is waking up. I wish I knew how to force myself up. Maybe some sort of physical trauma will work. I keep trying to hit myself and nothing works. This sucks. As I'm pacing to figure it out, I slip and that's what pulls me out of the dream and right to guards banging on the door.

I'm confused. Why do we have to go? I need more information, so I'll talk to the guards. I open the door and I'm met with 3 men at my door, one of them wearing a cloak behind the other two.

The front guard on the left speaks up, "Excuse me sir, we received information that there may have been a fugitive in the area. Would you know anything?"

"I haven't. Did everyone else get informed? There are children here in this building as well."

"No, we just recently got word about the fugitive and are trying to let the residents rest."

"So why bang on my door? Am I under suspicion?"

"No, but one of the two women you came with are." Oh damn, I know Chai steals things from time to time so she must have stolen something valuable to be on notice all the way out here. I ask, "What did they take?"

"Not take. It's what they are. They have alerted us to arrest all witches in the area." The guard responded

"Wait, you're looking for witches? What makes you think that either of them is a witch?"

The guard points to the hooded man and explains, "they have a special device that can detect large magic frequencies around them. They've been directing us for employment and it has been quite fruitful. We detected nothing in your room. We're just skeptical since you came with two women and they're gone, according to the Innkeeper." Damn, sounds like I was almost found out. I really would like to stay for at least a few more days to see what this city offers.

"Well, I'm sorry. I don't know where they went. I had paid for their room when they were sitting outside and looked cold, so unfortunately, your guess is as good as mine right now."

"That's a shame," the guard replies. "Well, we apologize for the inconvenience sir, goodnight." They close my door and head down the stairs. I feel bad because I can't let the girls know until later that I'm going to stay a while longer. I could try to conjure a bird and send it, but I don't know how to measure a 'large magic frequency.' Hopefully, the girls stay safe until I can get to them, but to not raise any suspicion, I should get some sleep.

The morning comes with no more strange dreams. I hope the girls are safe, but I'm curious if I can find anything to help me get stronger here. My primary goal is to get any sort of upper hand on Chairoi before we get to her school, so if there's even some shady backdoor teacher, I'm ready and able. Maybe if I take a walk around the city, I'll get some inspiration for training, but I'm starving. Hopefully, I can find a place to get some food quickly. After leaving the inn, I see several promising stores, but I see one store with a man meditating outside. Food can wait. I have a feeling that this could help with my training.

"Excuse me, sir." I speak up. He sits there, ignoring me. I tried again, "sir, excuse me." He still sits there, but this time, he points to the ground in front of him. I sat just so I could see what this was about. After about 15 seconds of some more silence, I said, "so, what's your name?" He taps my head and then suddenly, everything fades to black. It's like I'm in an entirely different realm.

"What would you like to know?" I hear from all around me.

"I could tell that you were taking your meditating seriously," I explained. "So I was curious if you could teach me the benefits of it. Like, is this whole thing just from constant meditation alone?"

He laughs, "No, not just that, but it helps clear the mind." The man suddenly appears before me, as if materializing from thin air. "My name is Kashifa, and I will teach you, but only because you seem to be the first person to maintain themself in this plane for a while."

"So what, you just tell people to sit in front of you and then you knock them out all the time?" I implied. "Isn't that weird?"

"I mean, I have a warning sign of sudden drowsiness at the top of my store," Kashifa mentions. "But you know, most people forget they can look up, I guess. Enough of that, though. The first thing we will speak about is being in tune with yourself."

I interject, "wait, so we're just going to do all of this in this random state of nothingness? We're not leaving this plane anytime soon?"

He explains, "This isn't just any plane of existence, this is inside our minds. I took you into my mind. That's why it is so calm and peaceful, but I have had training. Tell me when you are ready to be taken to your own mind, and be prepared to stand strong against any potential threats."

Potential Threats in my mind? What the hell is that even supposed to mean? If it's from me, then I should be able to handle it. "Alright, I'm ready!" He simply waves his hand and the calm landscape gets turned into a hellscape with fire and things that look like evil versions of my friends prepared to attack me. "Wait, what the-" Before I can finish the thought, the clone of Chairoi lunges forward with a powerful kick.

Kashifa gets me up to speed while he takes his leave to wherever. "These 3 represent your core emotions. The tall woman is your rage at yourself for still not feeling strong enough." After he says that, a giant fox tries to bite me, which I just barely get away from. It transforms into my brother. "Your sadness, as to feeling like no matter what you do, you can't give back enough to your community, and that you might lose them and never get them back." The last one is a clone of Alba, who actually doesn't attack me. Instead, she drops and whimpers, as if she is too afraid to be here. "And finally, your empathy, trying to understand others' pains, even if you have never experienced such hardships," he adds. "If you can't control these emotions, then you'll never be able to get to the next step in your training. So good luck handling them."

He's gone, and now I'm only left here with my thoughts and these three. He said I need to manage them, so maybe fighting them is the answer. I try to strike Chai with a blow, but I slip right through her as if she's a ghost, then she grabs me and chucks me across the room. What the hell??? How am I supposed to manage something I can't even touch? Chimer sends a flock of crows forward, covering me in them, before he pops out with an explosion to my face. For something in my head, this stuff feels very real. I look back over to Alba again, and she looks more terrified of my glance. He said I need to 'control these emotions' so maybe he meant I need to understand why I'm feeling this way, and how to better handle it than just ignoring it. I'm still getting bombarded by Chimer's long distance attacks and Chai's up close and in my face fighting style. I need to make this fight in my tempo rather than in theirs somehow, and I think Alba might be a crucial element. When we first met, she said I was different. That wouldn't mean much to me if it wasn't so obvious she was talking about men with how she acts around women. I think this version is still an Alba that's still afraid, so I need to show her that men aren't all terrible. Chimer drops his onslaught for a split-second and it gives me enough time to get Chai off me and run to Alba. "Alba, I'm here to help you!" I scream. She looks up with a face of hope at first, but it slowly turns to disgust and then rage as her eye glows.

"GO AWAY!!!" she screams, and it sends me hurling into spikes she forms right behind me. Yea, no shot, this is a dream because I definitely would have woken up from that. After she drops the spikes, I can't even let up for a second because Chai is right in my face with a swift roundhouse to send me flying and then Chimer forms a spiked coffin to catch me.

If I didn't know any better. I'd say you guys are trying to kill me," I jokingly say. Just then, I get swiftly hit in the back of my neck and drop unconscious.

When I wake up, I'm still in this alternate plane, but they seemed to have let me rest? "I intervened, don't worry." Kashifa is sitting here, waiting for me to rise.

"How long was I out?" I ask

"Don't worry, it was only about 5 minutes. You are surprisingly resilient, considering you took those spikes to the back twice, but I suppose you are one of *them*."

As I'm rising, I ask, "what's that mean? Are you saying that I'm some different species or something?"

"That doesn't matter as of right now. What does matter is you figuring this out," Kashifa assures me. "So, what do you think the answer to defeating them is?"

"I have to understand why they feel this way, and figure out a better way of managing them?" I say unconfidently.

"Unfortunately not," he says. "All of your emotions, your rage, your sadness, your empathy, give in to them. Once you fully embrace all your feelings you are bottling up, you will become one with yourself, and be in tune with your spirit." So that's what I've been doing wrong. I've been trying to put them in check, when I really should let them run free.

"Ok," I reply, "I think I'm ready for this. Put me back in."

Once again, I'm sent back into the hellscape, but this time, I ignore any sort of feeling telling me to hold it in, or hold back. I let myself go, and when I do, I let my body flow on its own. Any attack that Chai or Chimer sends my way not only cannot phase me, but I'm also able to connect on my own attacks. I understand it's okay to be angry and to let the rage fuel you. I understand that it's fine to be sad and the best way to handle it is by letting it all out. Crying can comfort you when you have no one else, and mourning is a natural process. After understanding that, they both vanish and Alba walks up to me. I understand that empathy is something that not everyone can have. Not everyone finds themselves in the same situation or can truly empathize with others, but it is possible to have sympathy, which is important for providing comfort to those who have experienced rare situations. It's not always a need, but sometimes it is a want.

"Thank you," she says while slowly fading along with this plane. Suddenly I jolt up. It hasn't even been 2 minutes in real time. "So, I see that you've done well. Come, we go just outside the city for you to learn this technique," Kashifa says.

"Can we eat first?" I say.

"Fine, we eat, then we go."

I'm feeling full, so now I'm more than ready. He takes me a ways out of the city, so far in fact, that I'm pretty sure it would be safe to set up camp here with Chairoi and Alba, so I might do that afterwards. "Alright," Kashifa chimes, "so I took you out here to learn a spirit awakening. Usually, I would teach you the first few steps, but since I know what you are now, I think it's ok to teach you the full technique: State of Oblivion. Since I see that your body can regenerate, then that means that your energy reserves should be able to as well. This State is supposed to use all the energy you have to output your body's current maximum potential and gives increased speed and the obvious damage output.

The usual drawback is that the longer you have this go on, the more your body dissipates, but you won't have this problem. So this entire state should honestly be easy for you to get to. What I want you to do is take a fighting stance."

Alright, simple enough. I take my stance. "Now, use your backhand to pinch your forehead, and then pull forward, but when you do this, have nothing on your mind to activate it correctly. When you gesture, I'll move out of the way, and then I want you to just give one punch directly into the air." Understood. I take a deep breath, I clear my head and then I give him the thumbs up to signal. I pinch my forehead, pull at it, then suddenly I feel my entire body boil as if I'm in a pot myself. Suddenly I go up into flames, and then just as fast, they simmer down, turning into steam around my body. I punch directly up into the sky, and the shockwave alone surprises me. "Try running around for a second," Kashifa says from a distance. I take one step, and I go at least 10 normal running steps. This is insane. I even output so much force that I'm able to propel myself into the air by just stepping. I fall back down and land away from Kashifa. "To deactivate it, either pinch again or think of something to calm you down." I pinch and I'm back to normal. What a strange way to go into a super powered state if you ask me, pinching a forehead. But at least I have something up on Chai the next time we fight.

"I appreciate this greatly. If there is anything else I can learn, I'm willing to listen," I say.

"Oh no, to be honest, I'm still a student myself. You seemed to be a quick learner considering most people take about 4-5 months to learn what you learned today." Kashifa assures me. Damn, I guess some things I'm just better at than others. It's been a while since I've talked to the girls and it is dark out, so I should get my things and then meet up with them, probably here. I bid my farewell to Kashifa and thank him for the wonderful lesson, then I send out Xander to find the girls as a bird as I go back to retrieve my things from the Inn. When I get back, my stuff is apparently missing, but the culprit didn't get very far. I see them just outside my window. To keep up in case they run, I jump out the window to follow them. I didn't account for how heavy I am, because they heard me and took off. They're pretty fast, and it makes me wonder if I should use that State I just learned, but I feel like it would be too much for a petty thief. Thankfully, a trap rope caught them and lifted them up while they were dropping my things.

"Well, you want to explain yourself?" I asked the thief.

"I just got told to grab whatever was in your room. Some guards paid me! I swear!." the thief pleads. What the hell would the cops want my things for?

"Whatever, just don't let it happen again." I say as I unhook him from the trap and let him be. It's even more weird that there's just a random trap set up right there considering that the city at least seems pretty safe, unless it was another thing set up to get me. I decide to head back, but waiting right around the corner is a group of guards, including the one that came to my room last night.

"Sire," one guard calls, "we become more suspicious of you with you not only coming to the Inn with two women who disappeared in the middle of the night with no trace, but also showing instances of public intoxication and clearly not being in the best mental state."

"Not the best mental state?" I reply in bewilderment. Are they implying that I was wondering about instead of just meditating when I was training? I felt looser, but I wasn't sure if it was all in my head or not.

"Please, it is in both of our best interest if you don't resist and come with us," the guard says while reaching to snatch me. I yank back and they all draw their weapons on me. This seems like a suitable moment to put this power to the test. I reach towards my chest and immediately get stabbed by all of them. I really need to figure out a more effective way of activating this, but I still force through the spears and activate the State, and break the spears while also moving myself to a nearby pillar to assess the situation better. This form gives me a boost in most physical abilities, but not so much to where they can't react. I'd say it's like the speed increase of a warthog or buffalo running, but I'm sure I can get closer to something like a cheetah with enough training. As we trade glances, there are only about 4 guards, and the sudden burst of speed seems to have surprised them. They're down a weapon in spears since it broke off when I moved, but they still have backup daggers, and I'd rather not get stabbed unnecessarily.

I dash in to incapacitate one with a swift blow to the exposed area of his neck, but right as I swing, it's blocked by some sort of invisible field. Just then, he swings at me, processing the situation. I dodge it, but the guard behind was expecting me to fall back and trip me, then plunge his knife down to stab me in the chest, with me just narrowly escaping.

One of the other guards yells, "What are you doing? You could have stabbed him right there and been done with it!!" The other guard responds, "he already broke our spears with his own freaking body, so I have a hunch: We either go for his heart or his head, then no chance he survives." This is a good idea to practice, especially since it's against competent fighters. I want to practice this and see if I can avoid taking any damage here. There's about 5 of them, with the one I tried to hit earlier staying in the far back. I might make a distraction by throwing off their focus using Xander and transforming him into something else.

"Hirundo!" As I say it, a swarm of birds surround me and disperse onto the group of guards. I use it as a chance to move behind the guard in the far back, and as I swing my arm again, it bounces off their body. What the hell is this, some sort of force field? As if wearing armor wasn't enough. By the time I refocus, he's already conjured up smoke blocking my vision. This is bad. Something else is in the smoke. Is it poison? I just know I feel my legs giving out, and it feels like the transformation is waning. I jump to the roof and, as I regain myself, I see the guards perched on an opposing roof with bows ready. It's almost like they have trained for exactly this moment, kind of weird. As they draw their bows, they shout 'FIRE' and I notice that their arrows have suddenly multiplied. I try my best to dodge or break them as they are raining down on me, but I'm hit by several, considering that I'm still woozy from the smoke. The guard ends up clamping some strange shackles on me with some sort of runic magic, and it shifts me out of my form.

"What the hell is this?!"

"You'll find out soon enough, don't you worry," the guard responds. As they make sure the shackles are secure, they place a sack on my head.

"What guards are you lot? This seems like you're planning for my execution."

"…."

They're dead silent, as if they are the ones in the terrible spot here. After about 15 minutes of them carrying me, I finally get placed on the ground and the bag taken off my head, just to be greeted by none other than Kashifa.

"What the-did YOU pay these guys to do this?"

"Don't be ridiculous. I pay them because I have to. It helps to always have an eye out, you know?" Kashifa says.

"What exactly do you mean?" I ask

"Well," he starts, "if you must know, this is Divine Adjacent Dining, or D.A.D for short. Basically, anything and everything that happens on Earth, we hear about whether it's big or small. When you were born, that was one of the major events we heard about because you are a UF."

"UF," I question. "Sounds like weird food."

"Individuals blessed with the ability to never die are called UFs, short for UnFading. You yourself have been in multiple life-threatening situations and when a normal human life would cease, you would regenerate. Am I right?"

"Yea, you're pretty spot on," I reply.

"BUT, I needed to bring you here because I need someone to keep an eye out on Alba. There's some strange energy coming off of her." Kashifa shifts his usual laid back demeanor into a more serious one. He even changes his posture from the usual slouch to sitting up straight. "If the energy that she's emitting is what I think it is, and it ever gets loose, there is no telling what kind of mayhem she may ensue."

"Okay, I get what you mean," I say, "But, I can also tell that whatever that energy is that we feel, it's not her. It is almost like she gives off two different people from one body, but she has shown nothing that would genuinely make me think that."

"You can believe whatever you want, but the council has their own concerns raised by her." He shuffles items around on the table and picks up some cutoff pink hair. "Someone left this at the location of a recently demolished building in Eastern Beirut. The only other things we found there included charred chunks of human flesh and tattered clothes for children. Now, I understand that there are many circumstances in her life that could have led her to do this, but this is far for a young girl from a small village. I need you to at least stay alert, and if anything happens, use this." He places a small sphere with a yellow insignia in my hand. "When you rub the yellow and whisper whatever you need into it, some of my men will come to assist you. I hope you're right about your feelings on Alba, but still better safe than sorry."

After I get a full night's rest back at the inn, I go searching for wherever the girls may be. I'm still stuck in this situation with Alba. Of course, everyone has the right to self-defense and to keep their own secrets. It just feels odd that she would randomly have so much faith in strangers so easily. She may not have been extremely open, but she seemed friendly enough.

About an hour of walking the opposite direction of the village, I can see some smoke lingering off the horizon, and when I finally reach the smoke, it's Alba and Chai.

"There you are!" Chai exclaims. "We were worried about you. Did they harass you, give you trouble, and force you to give up information about us?"

"Not really," I respond, "just more confused on where the two I was with had disappeared off to. But I learned some new techniques and was wondering if you want to test it out now."

"Not the best idea. I'm still drained and we've been sitting out here for a while with nothing to eat or drink. How far are we from Mount Kita anyway, Alba?"

Alba sits in silence for a bit, most likely using her familiarity to estimate the distance, "... about 3 days. So I know you say that you grew up in the mountains, but you mean around them...right?"

"No, I grew up **on** the mountains. There's enough flat surface that we have entire buildings constructed on them." Chai goes into detail, describing all the intricate designs, how some of the craftsmen almost lost their lives due to how the working conditions were set up and they had to all have a rope attached to them and the base of the site at all times in case anyone fell. It sounded both interesting and horrifying.

"Well, I am ecstatic about seeing this," Alba said, "But I am going to have to make a pit stop along the way again to your home Chairoi, because there's something I need to retrieve for my late mother. She said she left a vial for me to get at the 'edge of the world' so I'm assuming that's the edge of the land right before we cross over to your home. It shouldn't take me any longer than us just getting there and hopping over, so it will be really short."

Hmm, this must be the thing Kashifa was referring to, but we have to see it first before confirming any suspicions. For all I know, it could just be a final goodbye note. "I see nothing wrong. Let's get going then." Alba summons her dragon and we are off. While on the trip, I take out some of the extra rations I bought from the village before leaving and we enjoy a light meal with some conversations learning more about each other. Me and Chai are siblings while Alba was an only child. Our favorite time of the year is winter. Chai actually has three pets at home, one of them being a stoat with the two others being serows. When we discussed our profession, however, I was the only one who had a simple time describing their line of work.

"I'm a professional fighter. Whether I win-or-lose fights, I make a profit based on how many people come to spectate the fights." Utter silence after my statement. "Did I say something wrong?"

"No, no, it's just," Chai slowly begins, "I never really knew how to describe my job. I guess I'm a bounty hunter and an assassin. I have specific targets people give me to learn about, confiscate anything that was not originally theirs, and then, if I have to, eliminate said target by any means necessary. Sometimes, though, I let certain targets go because of personal feelings, I guess." That explains why she's so silent and nimble.

According to Alba, she is still just a student. "I never really got any education other than from the books I've read and that only started about 6 or 7 years ago, so I'm still behind. I still have so much to learn, so I hope that anything you can teach me along the way, you will." As she says this, she bows towards us as if she's begging for help. Suddenly, her dragon shakes. "What the hell? Someone is firing at us! How low was I flying?" As I lean over to see what she's talking about, there's an entire battalion that appears standing with bows drawn, aiming directly at us.

These aren't just standard bows though, because when they release, there's an explosion that happens after the impact. We get hit by about 60 before the dragon familiar dissipates and we plummet.

"Chai, quick!" I shout at her as she immediately recognizes I'm telling her to grab Alba. As I see her catch her, I exclaim, "Diomeda!" Summoning a giant bird that catches them and flies off into safety. As I fall, the last thing I can hear is Alba scream my name before losing consciousness.

The sounds of the birds chirping bring me back to wake. Looking around, the giant mountain that we were near isn't too far away. I must've been out for almost a whole day, if not longer. Not too far off, I can hear footsteps sprinting towards me, and a lot of them. As much as I would like to get up to defend myself, I'm still recovering from that drop.

"ရပ်လိုက်ပါ! မရွေ့နဲ့။" A guard shouts out something I can't tell, so I cast silver tongue. I got rid of Japanese because Chai has been teaching me the language in our downtime. The guards grab me by the arms and tie me up, restricting my arms and legs. "Our emperor would like to know what you are doing in our country," the guard explains, "so we're taking you to give him an audience." At least this means they don't plan on just killing me and tossing me to the side. I'm more confused about why they weren't concerned with how I survived a fall like that, mostly unscathed.

We walk for about fifteen more minutes before finally arriving at their empire. There were not only temples scattered on the way here, but there's practically a temple in every single corner I turn. They bring me not into any of the temples, but to a small house behind one temple, and untie my restraints. I'm a bit confused by this, but not unwelcoming of the sudden hospitality. The man who I can only assume to be their emperor comes from around a corner.

"Hello, my name is Kyiso. I'm so sorry for my men's aggression. They can never be too careful." He offers me a glass right after stating all this, "Tea?"

"No thank you," I declined. "I'm actually looking for my friends. We got separated on our way to a city off in the east. I believe it's supposed to be at the beach."

A few of the guards murmur to one another after I say east. "What is it?" Kyiso questions.

"It's just that," the taller guard says, "Far in the east, there's a tale of not only a world consuming dragon but also of a lot more beast that none of us are sure are even real, I'm sure you've heard of some tales before as well." He's not wrong. Some travelers have spoken to me about some of their hunts, and Chai has confirmed it as well. She told me she lost her arm fighting a beast that had the body of a snake but the legs of a lion and quarter the size of a mountain.

"Now that you mention it," Kyiso says, "there were some sightings by some residents of a strange beast not too far off our coast. It is towards the west, so if you aren't looking for any potential work, I understand. But if you are interested, I will pay you handsomely, and my men will accompany you to the coast, where it was last spotted." I could use this to fully test my new abilities. Blocking my breathing can disable my technique, so I need to come up with a solution to work around that. I also wouldn't have to hold back since it's a beast and not a human.

"Sounds good," I responded. "If your men wouldn't mind afterwards, could they guide me to the opposite coast as well?" Murmurs stir again.

"We would be more than happy to," answers the smaller guard, "but it is not our own territory, and we have a truce that forbids us from sending soldiers into each other's country unless we have received a prior message alerting us to a threat."

"Understood, thank you." I say. I'll just have to find another way to the coast. Kyiso offers me a place to stay and some food for the night, so I accept and use the time to read more of the wizardry books my brother gave me. Even though the books essentially aim to be grimoires, he offered me a book that focuses on various effects of mastering your spirit. I knew you could alter your body and increase your damage with it, but now I'm learning more about how to alter your ki into kinetic energy. That explains how Chai can move at speeds too fast for me to see, but I still have to learn how she diffuses the energy so fast. The next morning, after a hot bath, they provided an area for me to practice for a bit before we set off. I found out last night, there are also ways to manipulate your ki blast, so that's what I'm focusing on doing next and seeing if I can combine it with magic. The most efficient magic to use when I'm trying to be offensive is fire, but the best I've seen on the defensive is earth. Mixing my ki with water has also made me realize some healing properties are involved in spirit practice and now has made me curious to see if Chai could have regained her arm off of that method instead. Trying to use a normal ki charged blast doesn't seem to work for whatever reason, but I'm interrupted in my training.

"Sire, Sir Kyiso has requested an audience at once," the guard alerts me. We head over to see what the problem is.

"I have bad news," Kyiso says, "there seem to be some 'invaders' at the coast that have attacked our people. If you would be kind enough to go see them and dispose of these invaders and our monster problem, you will have immunity in our country, a place to stay in our best housing, and an even more handsome reward." He had me at a place to stay. I nod my head and wait to be briefed, but he tells me that everyone that's come to him has refused to describe what they look like. That's going to make this tough to narrow down, but I leave with the guards to guide me, anyway.

The emperor also gave me a compass to make sure none of us got lost and saw us out. We head out, but to give us a more straightforward path, we decide to stay on foot to avoid having to take the main road. It's about a 3-day trip if we don't sleep at all, but the trek takes about 5 days according to the two guards accompanying me, Champo and Htun. To make conversation, I ask them what made them join their royal guard. Champo explains he had actually planned on traveling the world, but he had already received training beforehand and the royal guard selected him because he was ahead of his group. Htun was not too far behind in the same training group, but is also the niece of their current emperor. They both have had nothing but nice words to say about Kyiso, and the entire country has been silent and calm as of late. Champo plans on requesting at least a month of leave to travel for a bit, with a desire to venture out further west. Htun seemed to have grown fond of Champo and said if he goes, she's planning to tag along. While the two are conversing, a tree drops in the distance, not too far from where we are. We all stand in defensive positions.

"Did you see anything?" Champo questions.

"Nothing out of the ordinary. How about you?" Htun asked.

"No nothing," I responded. "Stay alert though, they could wait for us to make the first move-" before I can finish, I'm snatched by one hand and shoved onto the ground. No matter how much I wiggle, I can't seem to move, but then my captor reveals their face and shushes me. I stop squirming when I hear monstrous footsteps passing by. Each step was louder than the last, big enough to not only leave a crater, but to decimate a town if they so much as tripped. We're hidden well in the bushes that are smothered in fruit juices to mask our scent, which is good because the first part of the beast that we can see is its nose. The beast is the biggest creature I've ever seen, the head alone the size of a home, and every step it takes is inches away from crushing us. It doesn't fully leave until about 10 minutes, partially because its tail is just as long as its body. When we know it's fully gone, my captor releases me and helps me up.

"Sorry about that. I didn't want you to end up like the last few guys we tried to help," my captor says. "My name's Sissel, as you can tell, I'm blind." He has a black blindfold covering his eyes and when he lifts it, his eyes are pure white. His hair is long and golden and a beard with two braids at the end. He's standing about even height with Chai, I believe, in a long Bearskin coat. "The other two are my twins that were assisting your friends." The twins in question come out, one with a headband covering his ears, and the other with a scarf covering his mouth. Both are about the same height as Sissel, and the crucial difference between them and him is that their hair is in a dreaded ponytail instead of loose and flowing. "The headband one is Kuuro, and the scarf is Mykkä. We ended up here somehow while searching for a cure for our village, which had a curse left on it." He walks over and gestures that he's made them get lost. "I may have gotten us lost here, but we have made progress in our search."

"Wait a second," I cut in, "how did you know he was-"

"Oh yea, so I use something that I've been calling 'Spirit Sensory'," Sissel explains. "How it works is that the ki within any living organism's body, I can see and use that for my vision. It also shows whenever their body gives off different emotions and leaves a certain aura around them. Hirviö gives off an immense amount of hunger, so I wasn't sure that even hiding in berries would keep us safe, but it seems it's carnivorous."

"I see. So, would you be willing to help us take down that thing?" I ask.

"Whoa, slow down now," Sissel says, "you're not ready for that kind of task yet. Not only does Spirit Sensory show me your ki, but it also shows your overall strength capacity. It also allows me to see your magic essence. The difference is it shows the ki welling up at your chest, and it shows magic welling up in your head. You have both signatures, but your ki is stronger than your magic and not by much."

"How much is not by much?" I questioned.

"Mykkä could beat you without nearing half his full potential," he says while gesturing to him to come over. Mykkä shakes his head and draws small wooden daggers. "They're training batons. He'll use these to remind himself that this is a sparring match. Let's see how you'll manage and then we'll work from there."

I look over at Champo and Htun. "You guys are fine if I take some time to train before we get going again?" They both nod their heads

"After seeing what we're up against, I'm in no rush, and will even spar with you," Htun says.

"Good, Mykkä, you can use the technique." As he says it, two more Mykkäs appear and ready themselves in front of Htun and Champo. "Same thing that goes for him goes for you two as well. Also, what's all your names?"

"I'm Zak, and these two are Champo and Htun. Alright Mykkä, whenever you're ready." I say. Before I can blink, he's already in front of me, and I have to duck before he swings. I see, it's going to be like how I fought Chai. Mykkä is never letting me get on the defensive and is constantly on the attack. I need just a second to activate the State of Oblivion, but I'm not being allowed any breathing room right now. Maybe if I envision it, I can activate it on demand. While still staying on guard, I try to imagine it happening, and as I foresee the chain being pulled, I burst into flames before they subside and I'm covered in steam.

"Interesting," Sissel says on the sideline, nodding his head. "Your ki more than doubled its original supply, but I still fear this may not be enough. Keep going Mykkä." Mykkä nods and then lunges at me, but I'm able to keep a more solid footing. I'm getting some hits now that I have amplified speed and more pack behind my punches, but it hasn't deterred Mykkä for a second. The hits I land don't seem to affect him at all, even though these would probably blow back a fully grown elephant. I throw a jab to get Mykkä to go low, which works, but when I go for the knee, he grabs me and slams me onto the ground, forcing me back into my base state.

"Damn, as I thought, you aren't fully using your potential," Sissel says. "I can tell you thought, 'since he's fast, I can out strength him' and you keep losing fights this way. He may be tall, fast, and slim, but that doesn't mean he's a pushover in the strength department. If anything, since he is moving that fast adds on to the power that he already possesses. Incorporate it more into your own attacks, use your speed to amplify your hits and also redirect your opponent's attacks with the speed they're traveling with into making them deal devastating damage to themselves."

After he gives me the breakdown, I take my stance across from Mykkä once again. He telegraphs a baton that's lunging for my head. I grab the baton and spin him around with his own momentum. He gives me a thumbs up, so I transform back into my SOB form and we pick back up the sparring match. It's now more even, neither finding an opening on one another. I can also feel that fighting with someone is helping me grow, even if we're both at a standstill at the moment.

After about 40 seconds, my movement is getting more fluid and my hits are getting even more potent to where I can see Mykkä is wincing when some of these hits land. He picks up the speed as well, trying to match me. Sissel is coaching Htun and Champo on what they should focus on as well, and when he looks over he tells us to keep going.

"You're closing the gap fast Zak, this form is helping you grow overall, but there's one downside that I'm realizing, I'll explain after you two finish," Sissel says. Is the downside he's referring to that this isn't my normal potency? I feel like I could sit in this form permanently if I wanted to, but just as I thought this, I get hit in the shoulder by the baton, which snaps my focus back, but too late. Mykkä wraps a baton around the back of my neck and shoves me onto the ground with it, shifting me back to normal again. Mykkä lets up his baton and backs up so I can sit up.

"I feel like the form is making you overconfident," Sissel says as he walks towards me and helps me up. "And you seem to hyper-fixate on other aspects besides the fight when you're in it. It's like your body wants to move autonomously, but when you're in that form, it makes you wander off. I think with how it amplifies your features, you should only use that when you plan on bursting your opponents down and ending whatever it is you're doing as fast as possible."

"So, should I pick back up sparring in my base right now?" I ask.

"No, spar with Champo and Htun right now instead," Sissel says. "I think in your current state, fighting someone weaker than you can still help you increase in strength, but it would have to be multiple at once, and I think your two friends fighting against you right now would do well."

So for the next 3 hours, I sparred against Champo and Htun and felt my strength growing exponentially. I was also moving a lot more freely over the course and understood what he meant by moving 'autonomously'. I also understood how Chairoi uses her ki for movement even more now, so I was using it to redirect some of their attacks at me. Afterwards, I asked Mykkä if he would like to spar again and told him this time to use his actual daggers. He agreed and me and Mykkä lined up across from each other for another bout. I used what I learned about ki-movement to be the one on the attack this time, landing a kick to the back of Mykkä before he could react. He swipes back at me, making me have to slow down for a second. He cast two clones, and they all jumped at me at once. I constantly have to dodge as I move around. Based on my knowledge of clones, usually striking the clone once will cause it to vanish, but delivering a hefty blow to the user will make all of them disappear. I'm still on the back foot, though. They aren't giving me any openings to take. Just then, the Mykkä on the left reels back for a second, so I jump towards him, and instead of attacking, I move right before my punch would've landed to get the other Mykkä to bump into him. They both disappear. So that would mean he wanted to divert my attention. I turn around to see if he's behind me, and end up feeling the wind just in time to block his attack from above. I break through, grab his hands, and slam him onto the ground, holding him down until he lets go of the daggers. Afterwards I helped him up, "thank you so much for sparring with me. This has been a great learning experience."

Mykkä just nods, and we head back to the rest of the group to have dinner before we sleep and head back out on our hunt. This is good to know that I've come this far though, especially considering it hasn't even been a month since I left home. While eating, Sissel explains some of his and his brothers' stories. Anything that's being said is being relayed back to Kuuro from Mykkä using signs with his hands for each word being spoken. Sissel also explains what exactly happened in his village and why they're here.

"We had just arrived back from looting a nearby villa, but a strange old hooded man had come." Sissel explains, "He was as tall as a house, and carried a Scythe. Initially, he stated that every person in the village owed a debt and he would wipe out the entire village. However, our persistent pleas and begging convinced him to make a deal with us. He told us that if we brought him back a flower, he called a 'Red Spider Lily' he would lift the curse off of our village. We didn't understand what he meant by a curse, but then suddenly a black mist covered as far as the eye could see, and when it lifted, everyone ended up with some sort of curse. I lost my sight, Kuuro his hearing, and Mykkä his voice. Other's in the village weren't so lucky, some of them lost limbs, others some organs, and about 15 out of the 200 of us lost their lives. Although my brothers may not approve of letting me navigate, the Red Spider Lily has a specific aura, and I can sense it in this country."

"Ahh, the spider lilies," Htun chimes in, "we have them growing in a garden close to our capital city. I'm sure that Emperor Kyiso would be more than happy to oblige and give your village whatever it needs to repay your kindness."

"This is great news!" Sissel jumps from his seat with excitement. "It's settled. We train for the next two days, and then we slay Hirviö. And you, my friend, will receive more than tenfold repayment for your kindness."

Following this, we will finish our dinner and rest. The next two days go by slowly, but the entire group sees a substantial amount of success in gaining power. I've gotten some better control over my powered up state and I understand how to turn my ki blast more effectively, and if I use it correctly, I can actually fly with it. Sissel and Mykkä both pointed out that my ki levels are actually higher than theirs by a large margin, but I was just never using it correctly. They're not sure why, but I know my ki gets stacked up on any time I 'die'. Instead of my body using ki to restore itself, it absorbs ki surrounding the air and tries to reconstruct it. But sometimes, there's an excess, which means my body uses what it needs, and saves the rest for later. This happens even when just mending my wounds. I'm not sure why my body absorbs it, but I have the equivalent to 8 human's worth of ki stored now. Even with all this power though, I'm nowhere close to being able to be at Sissel's level yet, but I am about even with Mykkä now, if not a tad bit ahead.

"This is good," Sissel says. "Everyone has made significant progress, Hirviö will give us a bit of trouble, but I'm positive that we can take it down, no problem."

"That's good and all," Champo says, "But how do you expect us to find it? With something of that size, you'd think they'd be a lot easier to spot, right?" Champo's right. We've been out here for about 4 and a half days now, and somehow, we've only seen the beast once, and afterwards, it disappeared into the wilderness. Sissel laughs and then walks over to Kuuro. Just his brother's presence lets Kuuro know what to do, so he raises his hand and a giant sphere appears, with an image of the beast inside it.

"We're always prepared, friend," Sissel states. "We've been keeping a watchful eye out on it. It's on the beach and it's been clear of any potential casualties, so we'll be taking the fight to it." Without a moment of hesitation, we rush towards the beach to finish this task. It feels like this training may have even improved our speed because we get to the beachside, which is supposed to be around 4 hours away, and we got here in 2 and a half hours. When we arrive, we can see the beast snooping its head into the water to find any food it can. We take this chance to get on the offensive and jump on it.

The first two stabs don't seem to phase it much, but Sissel jumps on top of its back with an ax that has burst into flames the second he digs it into its back, sending it reeling. With it standing on its hind legs, we get a better view of just how monstrous its size is. When it contacts the ground again, Champo loses his grip and goes flying back and Kuuro catches him before he contacts the ground too hard. Htun, Mykkä, and I are all focusing on a different leg to try to at least slow down the beast while Sissel breaks down its skin to open its weakest area. The plan is for me to switch spots with Sissel when the time is right and to go full power on it, but suddenly the beast sparks. Htun and Mykkä were the first to notice and jump off, but me and Sissel take the full brunt of the shock, getting electrocuted while still trying to hold focus. Kuuro sends a flaming arrow to the beast's eye, causing it to redirect its focus on us to him as he barrages it with more and more arrows, all with different ailments to see what has the best effect on it. While he does this, Sissel calls out to me and tells me it's time. I go into SOB and jump up onto its back, while charging my ki, aura grows all around me. I stretch my hands out in front of me, palms open, and release a blast of energy, but it seems to trigger the beast's innate defenses. It electrocutes itself again, stunning me and making me fall, slowly recovering myself while still being shocked. I hear Sissel shout from on top of the beast however, and see a massive beam of lightning strike down where he was before an orb zooms directly in front of me and he comes out of it, eyes glowing, hair a shade of light blue and his hand laid out, offering me help.

"I didn't think I would need this," Sissel says, "but it looks like I have no choice. Similar to your SOB, I have this form, but it's about 500 times stronger. In this I can no longer take damage, can become an essence of electricity, and I can also hit with my output being stacked by 350 times, but even then, this beast seems to be resistant to physical attacks. Your blast damages it, and we can't use this form forever, so we're going to try something. Hold my hand tight." As I grab his hand, we end up back on top of the beast in his exposed heart in the blink of an eye.

"His heart has a shell around it!" I shout to Sissel.

"That's why you're here," Sissel exclaims. "You are going to start back up your blast attack. When you hit it the first time, it started shocking because it peeled back its shell that was covering it. Even if I'm caught in the crossfire, both the blast and electricity won't affect me. When you peel it back, that's when I'll swing down onto it!" I nod and prepare my blast again. Jumping into the air, I place my palms forward, aimed directly at the beast's heart and Sissel. I release the blast, three times as potent now. I see the husk peeling back and see Sissel raise his ax, swinging it down so hard that I can feel the shockwaves in the air. The beast screeches, but has nowhere to run and cries out in pain until it stops. Such an arduous and massive task finished, and they said that it's been terrorizing their side for the past several years, but it's only been a few days. Me and Sissel dismount the beast's corpse and go to the group.

"I never thought I'd see the day," Htun says with a sigh of relief. "We had feared that the monster would go further inward and start just gouging on anything in its path. It's a relief not only seeing it defeated but also knowing that water was a necessity for it. It probably required a ridiculous amount, considering the size."

"That gives the idea. Maybe we could carve out some of it." Sissel says. "I'm sure it would taste good cooked, but we can also get scientists to study what this Hirviö is closest to in terms of the animal kingdom. Also, to find out where the hell it came from, as well as to show proof of our success." We all nod in agreement and begin carving away at the massive flesh. Obviously, we wouldn't be able to hold on to all of this meat, so we provide some to the local villages until all that's left are the bones. Since there's no proper way to dispose of the bones efficiently, we'll consider it a monument to our massive success. As we set up camp for the night before heading back, Sissel pulls me to the side because he wants to talk to me more in depth about my training.

"So, I'm sure you know about the 'rock-paper-scissors' of fighting, but do you know how there're levels?" Sissel asks?

"I knew about the '7 tiers' of magic, nothing about levels." I responded.

"I see," Sissel smirks. "Well, let me be the first to explain this. So each fighter has something that they focus on for their 'Spirit Style'. It's usually something you're born able to do, the same thing for magic, but sometimes, they can bleed over into other styles. Let's say, for instance, your innate ability has to do with speed and one level, from training, lets you trade off some of your speed for regenerative properties if you move normally for a bit. Someone with their innate thing being strength could have a similar trade-off situation. Sometimes, fortunate individuals are born with unbelievably strong powers, like the one you just witnessed. There's usually 5 levels, and that was me using the 5th, which took me YEARS to get to. So remember, train that power, or you won't be able to use its full potential and there is no guide. So make sure you keep that in mind and keep training, yeah?"

I nod my head, and we head back to the group. So there's five levels, which is what he said. I wonder if it's possible to go past that. Surely someone's already tried. My mind wanders off, focusing more on that talk and wondering how far I can get as we're eating. The next few days pass as we venture back to the Capitol. Emperor Kyiso welcomes us back with open arms.

"Ah, I see it was wise I sent my two most trusted guards," Kyiso says. "Both of you will receive handsome rewards for this."

"Well sir," Htun asks, "We'd like to know if we could go on a leisurely trip?"

"Hmm... I suppose I could make some arrangements...Very well, you may enjoy yourself for the next 2 months." Kyiso answers.

"THANK YOU SO MUCH, SIR!" shout Champo and Htun as they stand at attention and march out.

"Those two are quite cute. As for you, I see you've brought me friends." Kyiso says.

"Yes, they are the ones that helped me slay the beast, BUT I would like to say before, this one cannot hear, this one cannot see, and this one cannot speak." I say as I point to the brothers in the order they lined up.

"I see, well I appreciate your help and if there is anything I can provide, please let me know," Kyiso states.

"Actually," Sissel says, "we were told of there being a garden of Red Spider Lilies somewhere here. If it's not too much trouble, we would be grateful if we could take at least forty."

"Of course," Kyiso answers, "spend a night here and tomorrow morning, I'll have a shipment and a way to produce them yourselves for you. One guard will escort you and your friends to their chambers."

"Thank you," Sissel says, bowing his head multiple times as he exits the room. "You do not know how much this means to me. Your kindness won't ever go forgotten, my emperor."

"What a polite young man. As for you," he directs his gaze towards me. "I believe I have to uphold my part of the bargain, wouldn't you agree?" Kyiso asked. "We will leave at dusk to avoid any of the locals spotting me and two guards will accompany us. How does that sound?"

"Good for me, I guess," I shrug. Realistically, I could probably get to where I need to be if they just provide a compass, but this works fine, too. I've been training so hard for the past few days that I just use the remaining hours to rest. Walking around the city gives a bit more insight that it's a town for Buddhists, as if the over a hundred temples scattered weren't a dead giveaway. Some vendors in the area are offering rice noodle and egg meals. Considering I'm a tourist, I might as well taste what they're selling, so I give some coins and get some food. Conveniently, the currency used commonly around is penny and I have plenty from my fights. As I'm eating, some locals ask me what brought me to their country, and I tell them I'm just a nomad, venturing out further east. When one hears this, he tells me a story he heard while trading in China.

"People claim there is a crystal in the southernmost region that, if used correctly, can give everlasting life." The old man claims.

An older woman chimes in, "ah yes, I've heard of that. I believe it is called jade. It's also found in this country here as well, but I've heard it's more commonly found in China." Interesting. I believe Alba mentioned a crystal of some kind, so this must be what she is searching for. I wander around longer, but there isn't much to do here if you aren't coming for prayer or to speak to the emperor. As dusk rolls around, Emperor Kyiso comes to me in a carriage with some guards and directs me inside to discuss some important things with him on our trip.

"I am sure it has already come across your mind that it's strange that I've treated you with such hospitality," Kyiso says, pulling out a paper from the pocket of his robe. "My informants in D.A.D had told me I may have some visitors sooner than later, and full descriptions of each one." He hands me the paper and I read the descriptions of myself, Alba, and Chai.

Dazed, I ask, "Wait, just how much information does that group have on us?"

Kyiso responds, "It isn't just you, they have an extensive amount of information on everyone. The three brothers, for example, I knew about them from my D.A.D informants as well, so I knew they wouldn't be a problem. They also know exactly where you need to go to meet up with Alba and Chai, so that's where they're headed. They also informed me you have a new companion as well named Zhu-Li." Interesting. It was only supposed to be me and Chai, so it's strange that our group keeps growing in size, but it should be fine.

"How long should this ride take?" I ask.

"Usually about 3 days, including rest," Kyiso responds. "However, one of our guards has a special gift that will bring us there soon. We just had to make sure we were in a more secluded area." He peers out to check the surroundings and tells his guard to do it whenever he's ready. The carriage shakes, so at first, I thought we had gotten picked up and started flying. But as I look out the window, I see a flaming circle beneath us slowly rise, and as we rise through the circle, our entire surrounding changes. We go from traveling through the jungle to riding along the coast. Not too far off in the distance, I can see a city. Using the Spirit Sense technique that Sissel taught me, I'm able to see spirit and magic energy and the city has an unbelievably exorbitant amount of magic here that I assume is Alba.

"Perfect," I say. "This is exactly where I need to be. Did your informants let you know where my companions are, or was this a lucky guess?"

"They may have," Kyiso says slyly. "We can't venture any further since it isn't a political trip. I'll be making my leave, but I wish you all the best." As he says this, the carriage comes to a stop and I exit, bowing before leaving. As I head towards the city, I look back and see Emperor Kyiso for the last time as they go through a flaming circle back to where we came from.

The walk isn't terribly long, probably 30 minutes at most. When I arrive, I search for the largest producer of magic in the area. It brings me to a massive library and the first person from my group I can see is Chairoi. Standing right beside her is Albasayura and a woman sharing her stature, grabbing books off the shelf. The first to notice me as I'm approaching is Chai.

"ZAK!" Chai shouts as she runs towards me. The other two girls hear, and Alba follows behind Chai. "How have you been? Is everything ok? Where did you go?" Chai berates me with questions.

"I was in a neighboring country," I responded. "After I got shot down, their guards had taken me to their capital, and I met their emperor. They requested I help them with a task of taking down a hulking beast that was rampaging their coast. I believe it might've been like the same beast you spoke to us about, Chai."

Chai seems stunned for a second, and then speaks, "Impressive. That must mean your power has grown exponentially since our last bout. Well, I would like to introduce you to our newest companion, Zhu-Li. She claims to have traveled from far north of this country because an oracle told her about a woman matching Alba's appearance."

"A messenger spoke to me in a dream, originally," Zhu-Li chimes in. "They had told me I'm tasked with protecting and carrying out any request that Master Albasayura demands of me."

"Please stop calling me that," Alba says in an annoyed tone.

"Understood, my goddess," Zhu-Li responds.

"That reminds me, did you ever find the crystals you'd been looking for?" I ask Alba.

She shakes her head and responds, "It isn't jade crystals I'm supposed to harbor. After more research, and help from Zhu-Li, I need a jadeite. If I can get a more specific variation, red jadeite."

"I believe I have a workaround for this, but it will take some time, my goddess." Zhu-Li states. "For now, I think we should finish this trek that you three set out on to get to Chairoi's home. As long as we have time to spare, I can definitely get the crystals for you."

She seems rather confident, so we all nod and start traversing through the city. I inquire about all the events that have occurred in the past few weeks since we separated.

"After you sent us off on the bird," Chai explains, "we discovered an army believed to be under attack when they saw a giant beast flying, so they took to their defenses. It was also a perfect opportunity to test out their new weapons, as unfortunate as it sounds." We go to a tea shop and sit to eat and discuss more.

"So they were fine with you guys coming in with some magical being?" I ask.

"They weren't like the last place we stayed at," Chairoi explains. "Magic is not only welcome here, but they understand it's becoming more abundant as well as rising in terms of power and users. They'd rather get an understanding sooner than later, similar to my home country. Zhu-Li has even shown us books studying on the subject."

"They had even asked if I could teach them some tricks," Alba adds after finishing her tea. "I had to explain that it's very dangerous to use magic as if it is a toy. I then showed them how to make it look like your hand disappeared."

"Interesting. Well, let's get everything situated and get back on track. We still have to go to Mount Kita, remember?" I say and stand up from the table. The rest of the group follows suit. We paid for the restaurant, and they guided me back to the inn they were staying at.

"我想要一個單人房" Zhu-Li says. I never picked up the language, but I don't think I need to. I get my personal room right across from the springs for the night, and with how much has happened in these past few weeks, I decide to hop in the springs for a bit. Sitting in it isn't just to relax and rejuvenate myself, it's also to train. Being in the springs helps me clear out my headspace, which makes it easier to image train. Sissel mentioned that I apparently lose focus if I'm in the State Of Oblivion for too long, so I need to understand why. As I close my eyes, I imagine myself in a dark room, and I try to start off small, so my first opponent is Mykkä. I enter SOB and Mykkä spawns 3 clones. I try to ignore the clones and only focus on the original caster, so I have to keep weaving and blocking off the others. Mykkä and his clones speed up their attack. I'm losing my footing, and trying to split focus on clones, but stop myself and jump back.

I realize something, if Mykkä can create clones, then I should be able to do something similar. I take a deep breath and focus. As I'm shaking violently, a second of myself splits outside of me, a clone, but using a different technique than Mykkä. I used my energy and multiplied my atoms, creating a second of myself, but I could tell it was not at full strength. It has my same increased speed, and the aura that burns almost everything in its radius. I practice with this and see if it fairs any better than fighting solo versus 4, and it is showing better results. It's easier to fight two people and the clone shares my fighting knowledge as well, so it's dodging well. The only downside is that Mykkä still isn't showing any openings. Since me and the clone share a brain, I try to make a combo play by having the clone hold them off as I charge up an energy blast. Unfortunately, the clone can't hold them off long enough before they break through and stop me from charging. I have to figure out a better strategy, or understand what I'm doing wrong. Maybe there's a way I can empower myself more? I go through the different magic arts that I've learned.

      "You are overthinking it." I hear a voice come from behind me in the darkness. It's…Chimer? "You tried to learn every single art, but you should focus on a specific area. For example, I focused on the summoning arts. I can create constructs of not only small and large animals, but even foreign beasts not of this realm. And if I really wanted to…" He flicks his hand lightly and suddenly clouds form. I thought this space to be an infinite void, yet suddenly, an entire landscape appears. My brother and I stand at the top of a mountain while lightning strikes from the clouds all around. A thunderous screech almost makes me lose my footing.

"I choose to keep this level of my powers hidden because there's no use to the destruction it could cause," my brother says. The beast hidden in the clouds flaps its wings once, sending me almost flying before my brother uses his magic to catch me and once the massive gust of wind is gone, I look at the 'thing' before me. A bird that makes the previous beast we fought look like a light meal for this gargantuan being. It has lightning blazing all around and if it really wanted to, it could probably eat an entire village in once singular swoop.

"This is what you can achieve if you stop trying to be a jack of all trades and decide to be a master of one," my brother states. "I could even absorb it and give myself all of its traits."

"How the hell would you know that?" I ask "How did you ever even know you could summon it? I feel like I would've seen something that big!"

"Just like you train here," Chimer says, as the room goes back to being a black void, "I have my void for training. Once you get to that level, you'll understand. Back to the task at hand. What do you want to focus on, improving specifically in magic?"

I contemplated for a bit. Then I respond, "I think the smartest option for me would be blood magic. I have an infinite amount of blood, so I can use the full potential of it without ever having to worry."

My brother nods, then says, "Alright. The first thing I want you to do is clap your hands together and

aim them at me, palms sideways." I do exactly that.
"Now, you are going to imagine the blood pulsing out,
firing directly at me." I try to focus on doing it, but it's no
good. I power out of my SOB and try once again, but to
no luck. "Remember, use your brain for magic." My
brother mentions, while pointing at his head. "The power
is all mental. When you blast out the blood, it seeps
from your pores. It doesn't require an open wound." I
consider what he said and try again. But this time, blood
shoots out from my index finger. Right as the blood is
needling towards Chimer, it curves around his head and
goes straight into the floor, splattering a pool of blood. I
retract my hand and the blood stops piercing out.

      "Usually," my brother begins, "You wouldn't be
able to do anything special when starting at the first tier
of your art, but I've enabled you to see some growth
within the next few years now that you started, albeit
late. Try to add this into your next spar with Mykkä now
and let's see if you can see the special technique as
well."

      "Wait, how are you even here?" I ask.

      "When you get as strong as me, you can be
anywhere." Chimer responds, smugly.

      I scoff, but then readjust my attention again to
Mykkä and the clones that have come back into focus.
Instead of going into SOB, I created three clones and
have them use SOB instead while I focus on the main
Mykkä. Mykkä tries to get the jump on me by rushing in
with a swipe at my head with his daggers, but I duck and
weave out the way. I try to shoot him back with a blood
piercing, but he blocks it off of his daggers. I'm curious

though, even though it is out of my body, can I still control it? He tries to sweep me off my feet, but I jump and use a blast to push myself back so I'm not wide open in the air. But I infuse this blast with my blood, which covers him with blood. I try to summon small spikes to see if I can stun him, but I end up giving him blood-covered spike armor. I'm still getting used to this power, so there are definitely some flaws. As he runs at me, I try the spikes again and I end up using the blood to puncture his vital points, leaving him incapacitated.

"You're getting the hang of this," Chimer says. "I think we've had enough training for now. You should rest and get ready for your trip tomorrow." Chimer walks behind, pats on my back and I come back to the springs. I look around, but no one else is even close to me in the area. Strange, I guess he really is that powerful. I get out and rest in my room to prepare for whatever tomorrow throws at me.

Banging on the door wakes me up. I get up to go check and it's Chairoi.

"Everyone is all ready to go. How much longer do you have?" Chai asks, rushing me.

"Well, I did just wake up, give me a bit, and then I'm ready to head out," I responded.

After I gather all my stuff together, I go meet up with the girls right outside the inn. They go around saying their goodbyes to the friends they've made here and we get to the edge of the city. Alba cast her dragon, and we all boarded, but I'm getting a distinct feeling than usual from the group.

Chairoi is understandably excited since she's going back home, but I get a feeling of unease from Albasayura. I would check on her, but Zhu-Li is currently berating her with questions such as, 'does she need a foot massage?' So I think I'll leave her be for now.

"It's fine Zhu," Alba bluntly says. "This should be a rather fast trip if I'm not mistaken, so expect to be home sooner than later, Chai." The realization of what's going to be happening soon is finally kicking in and I'm realizing just how far from home I really am. I don't think I'm getting homesick, but this distance makes me miss my old friends and day-to-day more than I realize. But then I remember that's what this is for. So when I get back home, I'll never lose a fight and can protect my village from anyone and anything, no matter what. The next time my village sees me, they'll know that I'll be even further past Chimer's status.

I don't realize how exhausted that sparring session had made me. I kept phasing in and out of sleep. With the brief vision and hearing I can muster, I see the mountains coming up in the distance with a beautiful small town spread across them and I hear Chairoi's voice say, "Welcome to your new home for the next 5 years!" before I fully pass out.

To Be Continued in UnFading: Echoes of The Past

www.ingramcontent.com/pod-product-compliance
Lightning Source LLC
Chambersburg PA
CBHW020638130626
46552CB00003B/1296